DEATH
and DYING

Carol Antoinette Peacock

Franklin Watts
A Division of Scholastic Inc.
New York • Toronto • London • Auckland • Sydney
Mexico City • New Delhi • Hong Kong
Danbury, Connecticut

Dedication

In memory of my father,
Andrew Clinton Peacock

Cover illustration by John Gibson.
Interior design by Kathleen Santini.

Library of Congress Cataloging-in-Publication Data

Peacock, Carol Antoinette.
    Death and dying / Carol Antoinette Peacock.
        v. cm. — (Life balance)
    Includes bibliographical references and index.
    Contents: Grief, a normal response to loss—The work of grief—
    Warm up—Heavy lifting: expressing the feelings—Getting extra
    help—More heavy lifting: keeping memories alive—Moving on.
        ISBN 0-531-12370-7 (lib. bdg.)   0-531-16728-3 (pbk.)
        1. Grief—Juvenile literature. 2. Bereavement—Juvenile literature.
    [1. Grief. 2. Bereavement.] I. Title. II. Series.
        BF575.G7P3783 2004
        155.9'37—dc22
                                                    2003019765

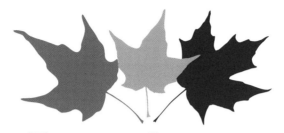

TABLE OF CONTENTS

One

Grief Up CLOSE

Eleven-year-old Carrie came home from school to find an ambulance and two police cars in front of her house. She watched as medics carried her father out on a stretcher. The sirens blared, and the ambulance sped her father to the hospital. Carrie's father died of heart failure several hours later. She never even had a chance to say good-bye.

Carrie couldn't believe what had happened. "I was in a daze," Carrie recalls. "How could my father be dead, I kept wondering. It didn't make any sense."

For weeks after her father's death, Carrie couldn't sleep. She was so sad that she cried until the sun came up. Each morning, Carrie stayed in bed, too exhausted and too depressed to move. She lost her appetite and went for days without eating. When Carrie went back to school, she avoided her friends because she didn't want to talk about her father. She dropped out of the school play and quit the soccer team.

Carrie couldn't focus. Her grades suffered. She began to have fainting spells and get bad headaches. Sometimes she threw up. Carrie even found herself looking for her father at the breakfast table where he usually sat. Sometimes she called out for him.

Carrie was not herself. She was afraid she was going crazy.

What Is Grief?

Carrie's responses to her father's death are part of what we call grieving. Grief is a natural response to loss. It is the way people react when they lose someone they love.

To understand grief, let's start with loss, which triggers grief. Most people experience some form of loss early in their lives. First losses can include the loss of a beloved teddy bear, the loss of a tooth, or even the loss of parents' undivided attention when a brother or sister is born. For young people, the most common losses, in order of likelihood, are:

• Death of a pet
• Death of a grandparent

- Parents' divorce
- Moving (loss of familiar home, neighborhood, friends)
- Death of a parent or sibling
- Death of a friend

Of all the losses you will experience, the death of someone you love is one of the most difficult. Grief is painful for everyone. Young people grappling with grief for the first time are often confused and frightened. Like Carrie, they may fear they are going crazy.

Your Grief Journal. *Throughout this book, we will suggest writing exercises and activities to help you handle your grief. Find an old notebook, or buy a special one covered in fabric or shiny paper. Keep your Grief Journal in a private place so that you can write freely, whenever you wish.*

Grief expert Earl A. Grollman, a writer and rabbi, has spoken with thousands of young people about how to cope with grief. "When you lose, you grieve," he writes. "Like all people who suffer the loss of someone they love, you are going through a grieving process. Grief is unbearable heartache, sorrow, loneliness. Because you loved, grief walks by your side... Grief is not a disorder, a disease, or a sign of weakness. [It is] the price you pay for love."

Three Levels of Grief

We tend to think of grief as a set of feelings, particularly sadness. Actually, grief is more than a feeling. Grief can strike people on three levels:

- Physically—grief appears in our bodies
- Emotionally—grief appears in our feelings
- Behaviorally—grief appears in our actions

Physical Signs of Grief

People who are grieving may suffer from a range of physical symptoms, including stomachaches, chest pains, dry mouth, nausea, and digestive problems. Usually, these ailments are caused by grief-related stress. Stress is our body's response to change or danger. When we're under pressure, our bodies go on alert. Stress hormones pour into the bloodstream, preparing us for action. Our pupils get larger and our muscles tense. Breathing becomes rapid. Our heart speeds up. Our blood pressure rises as blood rushes to the brain and muscles. We sweat to cool down our straining bodies.

Stress that persists over a long period of time creates chronic fatigue, muscle aches, digestive difficulties, breathing problems, headaches, back pain, and sleep problems. Stress also weakens the immune system and makes people vulnerable to colds, flu, and other illnesses.

THE SIGNS OF GRIEF

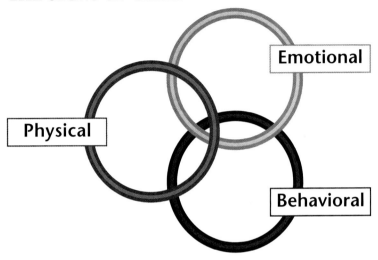

Grief can strike people on three levels. Problems in one area may also affect the others.

One of the top causes of stress is grief. In 1967, stress experts Thomas Holmes and Richard Rahe developed a Stress Scale for Youth, ranking forty-nine stressful events experienced by young people. The death of a parent or friend was rated as the number-one source of stress.

For a person new to grief, the physical reactions brought on by stress can be alarming. As grief subsides, however, these signs usually lift and the body returns to normal.

Emotional Responses to Grief

Interestingly, many people's first emotional response to

loss is to shut down and feel nothing. This numbness helps people protect themselves from feelings that are too difficult to absorb right away.

After the first days of shock and disbelief, grief can generate a whole new set of feelings. In 1996, psychologist J. William Worden studied 125 children aged six to seventeen, all of whom had lost a parent. His research, called the Harvard Child Bereavement Study (HCBS), was the first that involved speaking with the children themselves, rather than their parents or teachers. The HCBS was also longitudinal, which means that the children were studied for a two-year period, starting at the time their parent died. This approach provided information about how their grief changed over time. Based on his research, Worden reported that grieving children experience four common emotions: sadness, anxiety, guilt, and anger.

Sadness. In the HCBS, children who had lost a parent reacted with sadness and tears when they learned of their parent's death, and two-thirds cried again sometime during the first few weeks. One year later, 13 percent of the children were still crying daily or weekly. Worden reports that crying and sadness could be sparked by seeing others cry or by missing activities shared with the deceased parent.

Anxiety. The HCBS revealed that bereaved young people experience great anxiety—especially, in the case of a parental loss, about the safety of their remaining parent. Anxiety and worry are a normal part of grieving. For young people, fears may include:

- How will I survive without the deceased (the person who has died)?
- Who will be there for me?
- How will my life change?
- How can I go on with my life?

Guilt. Many of Worden's subjects admitted feeling guilty following the death of a parent. Guilt tended to focus on time not spent together or on words not spoken. One boy in Worden's study, who was eleven when his mother died, felt guilty that he talked back to his mother when she was alive. Two years later, he was still tormented by guilt. "I never said 'I love you' to her. Now, I wish she could be back and I could say it. Maybe when she died, she didn't know."

Anger. Many of Worden's subjects, particularly boys, also felt anger, most often about a year after a death. The young people in Worden's study expressed anger at God for letting their parent die or at the parent for dying. Anger is a normal response to death.

In addition to the four major feelings of sadness, anxiety, guilt, and anger, people experience other feelings, too. Grieving people may experience mood swings, helplessness, loneliness, and apathy. Sometimes, if the person who died was suffering or had been abusive to the deceased, the grieving person may feel relief.

Behaviors of Grief

Joe's beloved basketball coach was killed in a hit-and-run car accident while driving home from practice one night. When his best friend called with the news, Joe was devastated. But at the funeral, Joe didn't cry. He felt, instead, a tightness in his chest and a heaviness in his legs.

Joe took a week off from school and stayed in his room, most of the time listening to music. He picked fights with his younger brothers and sisters. Once, he threw a lamp against the wall. When he returned to school, Joe was edgy. Usually polite, he was now sarcastic to his friends and rude to his teachers. He even got into a fistfight in the bus line.

People who are grieving often act in ways that are different from how they usually behave. At home, young people may cry endlessly, have angry outbursts, or withdraw from their families. In school, young people show problems with concentration, restlessness, and poor academic performance. Sometimes, they revert back to behaviors characteristic of younger children, such as temper tantrums or stuttering.

Grieving people may also dream intensely about the deceased, call out to the deceased, talk to the deceased, or find themselves searching for the deceased in shared or familiar places. Grief experts call these kinds of behaviors "searching and calling out" activities. The behaviors associated with grief usually correct themselves as grieving proceeds.

Grief Journal Exercise: *To clarify your grief reaction, list the ways you are responding to your loss emotionally, physically, and behaviorally. Use this exercise as a springboard to other writing about your grief.*

Grief Is Unique

Consider your fingerprint. It is unique and different from everyone else's fingerprint. Grief is the same way. With each loss, we have our own special "grief print." Grief is shaped by many factors, including the quality of your relationship with the deceased, the nature of the death, your personal style of coping with stress, and the extent of your support system.

Other factors, such as your age, can influence your grief. Young children under five, for instance, do not understand that death is final. They often have trouble eating, sleeping, and controlling bodily functions. Children aged six through nine are curious and confused about death. They may become afraid of school, have learning problems, develop aggressive behaviors, or express concern about their own health.

ANIMALS GRIEVE, TOO

Studies have shown that animals are capable of experiencing some of the same feelings that humans do, including grief. In 1996, the American Society for the Prevention of Cruelty to Animals conducted a Companion Animal Mourning Project. The study revealed that 66 percent of dogs that had lost a dog companion exhibited behavioral changes, including eating changes, sleep disturbances, and clinging behaviors. Eleven percent stopped eating altogether.

But it's not just dogs that grieve. World-renowned animal researcher Jane Goodall spent years studying a group of chimpanzees in Tanzania. In 1972, one of the chimps, a mother named Flo, died. After her death, Goodall reported that Flint, Flo's eight-year-old son, sat over Flo's body for hours. He tugged at his mother's hand. He climbed a tree and stared at the nest where he and his mother had slept. Flint became increasingly listless and died in less than a month.

Cynthia Moss, who studies wild African elephants, reports that mothers who have lost a calf trail behind the rest of the elephant family. Elephants also linger over the bones of deceased family members, picking them up and carrying them some distance. Behaviorists speculate that the elephants are somehow remembering those who have died.

By age ten, young people grasp the finality of death. They may experience guilt, anger, and shame, as well as increased anxiety over their own death. Changes in eating habits as well as a loss of interest in outside activities are common. Teenagers may fear that their grief will make them different from their peers, and think that relying on adults for comfort will prevent them from growing up.

Gender Differences

Your gender can also shape how you grieve. Women and girls are generally more open with their emotions, including those of grief. They may, however, have difficulty verbalizing anger. Men, on the other hand, can deny their feelings and may have trouble expressing their grief.

Grief, then, is a natural response to loss. Newly bereaved people are relieved to learn that their responses—emotional, physical, and behavioral—are all a normal part of grief. Reassured, they can proceed with the grieving itself.

Grief Journal Exercise: **List or describe the factors that make your grief special and unique to you. Write about your relationship with the deceased.**

How People

Two

GRIEVE

K evin's grandfather died of a stroke at age ninety-three. He had lived with Kevin's family since Kevin's parents got divorced years earlier. Deeply upset about his grandfather's death, Kevin resented other people's reactions to his loss. "At the funeral, people said, 'Well, he had a good long life; it was for the best.' For the best? How could the death of my Grandpa be for the best? Some people said, 'Be happy for him; he's in heaven.' I'd rather him be at my baseball game, not in heaven. A few people said, 'Your mother loved her father; try to help her now.' How could I help my mother when I felt so bad myself? What did any of these people know about anything?"

Myths About Grieving

Society urges grieving people to put their grief away and move on. Well-meaning friends often try to protect the bereaved person from the raw feelings of loss with statements that encourage the griever to stop grieving. The myths that surround grieving can be dangerous, because they derail the grieving process.

Myth	Fact
"Let's change the subject. Talking about the death will just depress you."	Grieving people need to talk about their loss to start feeling better.
"Time heals all wounds."	Time itself does not heal wounds; it is what you do with the time that matters.
"You should be happy. The deceased is in heaven."	Unless the deceased was suffering terribly, it is unrealistic to expect to be happy after the loss of a loved one.
"It's time to get on with your life."	There is no timetable for grief. For bereaved people, grieving is their life.

Guidelines for Grieving

When you learn a new sport, a coach teaches you the rules. When you take up a musical instrument, a teacher shows you how to play the notes. People facing grief for the first time, however, are given few lessons about how to grieve or what to expect. Many young people who've had little exposure to grief discover that they don't know *how* to grieve.

Some grieving people worry that because they are numb, they cannot grieve or don't really miss the deceased. Others are anxious because they think they "should have gotten over it by now." Grieving people may also fear that if they let themselves feel the emotions of grief, they'll fall apart completely. Here are some guidelines about grieving.

There is no right or wrong way to grieve. People grieve differently. As the students in one fifth-grade class learned, there is no "correct" way to grieve. Everybody in class knew that Will had a childhood cancer called leukemia, but nobody talked about it much. One day, the teacher, Ms. Matrisciano, told the class that Will had died in the hospital the previous night. Everyone was stunned.

Over the weeks that followed, the students all grieved in their own way. Some put the death quickly behind them, seeming to go on with their lives. Will's homework partner, Janelle, was sad and didn't talk as much in group discussions. Ben, Will's locker mate, grew sullen and angry.

The grieving process ebbs and flows. Some people, especially young people, grieve in "spurts." A certain song or memory may release a flood of grief feelings. In Ms. Matrisciano's class, for instance, Will's best friend, Jacob, grieved most on Tuesdays, the day of band practice. Jacob and Will had both played the clarinet and shared a music stand. "Every time I played my clarinet, I felt a big knot in my throat. I could hardly go on because I missed Will so much," Jacob remembers.

Grieving has no timetable. Grief experts suggest that the most intense reactions to a death may come during the first two weeks and that the first year can be the hardest. Anniversaries and holidays may bring back the sadness, even briefly, for the rest of your life. Grieve at your own pace and don't pressure yourself by expecting that you will feel better after a certain amount of time.

Grieving as Work: What the Experts Discovered

In 1917, the famous psychologist Sigmund Freud wrote an important paper about grief. He described "the work of mourning," as the way people withdraw the energy they had attached to the deceased and begin to live without that person. By introducing the concept of grieving as work, Freud set the stage for grief experts to come.

Twenty-five years later, a tragedy in Boston triggered another significant breakthrough in the understanding of grief. On November 28, 1942, after a football game between two rival colleges, fans went to the Cocoanut Grove nightclub to celebrate. A fire swept through the club, and 492 people died. Thirty-nine burn victims were brought to Massachusetts General Hospital for treatment. Patients who had lost family and friends in the fire were counseled by a staff psychiatrist, Dr. Erich Lindemann.

Lindemann interviewed 101 bereaved people, including survivors of the Cocoanut Grove fire and their close relatives. In 1944, Lindemann described the symptoms of normal grief and other less-typical grief reactions. He also coined the famous term "grief work," the process of letting go of the deceased, adjusting to life without the deceased, and forming new relationships.

Several decades later, in Chicago, Swiss-American psychiatrist Elisabeth Kübler-Ross also interviewed hospital patients. Unlike Lindemann's subjects, these patients were not bereaved; they themselves were dying. In 1969, Kübler-Ross published her world-renowned book, *On Death and Dying*. Kübler-Ross's study concluded that all dying people progress through five stages: denial, anger, bargaining, depression, and acceptance.

Kübler-Ross's Five Stages of Coping with Dying

Stage	Typical Expression
Denial	"Oh no, not me. It can't be true."
Anger	"Why me?"
Bargaining	"Yes, me, but..." and "If only I could live to see..."
Depression	"Yes, me." (sense of great loss, past and present)
Acceptance	"It's okay." (patient is almost devoid of grief feelings)

Today, some people question Kübler-Ross's research methods. Others contend that dying people are unique and do not follow a universal model. Nevertheless, Elisabeth Kübler-Ross remains one of the foremost writers in the field of death and dying.

In the 1970s, grief counselors applied the Kübler-Ross stages not to the process of dying but to the process of grieving itself. Some grieving people find Kübler-Ross's predetermined steps a useful tool as they track their movement through grief. Many people, however, experience grief as a roller coaster, not as a neat progression from one well-defined level to another.

The Tasks of Grieving

Kübler-Ross's research rekindled interest in how people grieve. Grief experts took a new look at the notion of grief as work, the idea first proposed by Freud and Lindemann. Worden and others devised specific tasks for grieving adults and children. In 1988, death educator Dr. Sandra Fox, founder of the Good Grief Program in Boston, proposed four clear tasks for small children and their caretakers. These tasks began by helping grieving children understand the concept of death.

Unlike small children, young people age ten and over understand the concept of death and need their own plan for grief work. The following steps are based on Fox's tasks but are geared specifically to young people. These tasks can be done in any order, at any pace. They invite the grieving person to get active, take charge, and feel better.

- **Warm up.** This is a preparation phase. During "warm-up," grievers learn about the typical signs of grief. They plan ways to take care of themselves physically and to identify people who can provide support.
- **Express the feelings of grief.** During this stage, people communicate grief feelings in words or in other ways, such as writing, art, or music.
- **Honor the memories.** During this stage, people find ways to keep the memories of the deceased alive.
- **Move on.** In this final stage, people begin to feel better.

Although grief work ultimately helps people to feel better, many grieving people cannot imagine taking on these tasks at first. When twelve-year-old Kayla's mother died of multiple sclerosis, a nerve disease, Kayla's grief was bottomless. Later, a well-meaning relative suggested Kayla would feel better if she did grief work. "Grief work?" Kayla fumed. "I could hardly get up in the morning, much less do some sort of work!"

It may help to remember that grief work is a joint undertaking. Grieving people can call upon family, friends, and professionals to help. Grief work is also empowering.

Many people who begin the tasks of grieving find relief when they take action. One of the terrible feelings of grief is helplessness. Through grief work, bereaved people can regain some measure of control.

Finally, grief work works. The most compelling reason for taking on the tasks of grief is that they are effective. By shouldering these tasks, even people new to grieving have a plan for confronting their grief and feeling better.

Grief Journal Exercise: *Set aside some pages in your journal for an Action Plan, where you can record the steps you take as you begin your own grief work. Keeping track of your progress will help you feel proud of tackling even the smallest tasks.*

Three

Warm Up

Grieving is like running a marathon. Most runners warm up for the race ahead. They gather a team of fellow runners to train with or a group of friends to cheer them along the route. Runners also take good care of their bodies so that they can endure the rigors of the race.

To prepare for the grieving ahead, you, too, need a support team, a group of people you can count on. Like a runner in training, you can also work hard to stay healthy. Grieving requires stamina. Because grief is often expressed in our bodies, we can begin to ease our grief—often for the first time—when we care for ourselves physically.

Toolbox for Grieving

People who are grieving may want to gather a set of "tools" to help them get started:

- *A journal.* Your grief journal can be a special book or an old notebook.
- *A calendar.* This could also be a daily or weekly planner, where you can write down your exercise routine, appointments with friends, and so on.
- *Tissues.* Crying helps.
- *A notepad or sticky notes.* Use these to communicate with the adults in your life. A note could say, "Please get more milk" or "Don't forget that I have soccer practice tomorrow."
- *A list of phone numbers.* This list should include people you can call if you're feeling lonely or need something.
- *A library card.* Use this card to check out some books about grieving.
- *A computer (or access to a computer).* A computer can help you check out Web sites about grief.

Your Support Team

People who are grieving need others they can turn to during the hard times ahead. For many grieving people, the person they've lost is the very person they relied on in times of trouble. "I could always go to Grandma," said Jenny, whose grandmother died from head injuries caused by a fall. "Whenever I needed to talk, Grandma would make me a cup of cocoa and we'd sit together on her rocker. I could tell her anything. So when she died, I went straight for her rocker. Of course, it was empty."

Often, when a young person is grieving, the people in his or her life may also be consumed with their own grief. The death of a parent can leave the other parent emotionally paralyzed and unavailable to the children in the family. For this reason, it is a good idea to take stock of the people who are able to help. Your support team could include:

- Your immediate family
- Your extended family (grandparents, aunts, uncles, etc.)
- A family pet
- Adults at school or in extracurricular activities, such as a teacher, guidance counselor, etc.
- Friends
- Neighbors
- Your family doctor
- People in religious organizations, such as your minister, rabbi, priest, or youth group

Grief Journal Exercise: In the Action Plan section, list the people on your Support Team. In another column, note specifically how each person can help.

People help in different ways, depending on their role in your life and their relationship with you. Members of your support team could offer an ear for listening, hugs, help with staying physically healthy, a diversion from sadness, and prayer or spiritual thought.

A Support Wheel

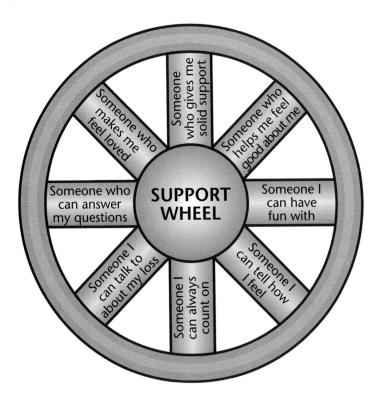

Determine which people in your life can offer support in the areas listed above.

Pets for Comfort

Researchers report that bereaved people often turn to their pets for solace. Stroking a pet lowers blood pressure, reduces anxiety, and promotes a sense of well-being. Additionally, pet owners report that their pet's unconditional acceptance and emotional responsiveness provide comfort and reassurance in times of stress.

Getting Started: It's All Connected

Thirteen-year-old Jasmine admired her older sister, Peg, who took her to movie matinees and to all-you-can-eat buffets at the local Chinese restaurant whenever she visited. On one trip home, Peg was killed in an airplane crash.

Jasmine was devastated. At night, she felt so sad that she could not sleep. Sleep deprivation created its own set of problems, including mental confusion and irritability. Exhausted and unable to focus in class, she began to fail in two subjects.

Jasmine's response to her sister's death shows us that people's grief responses are interconnected. For Jasmine, an emotional response (sadness) led to a physical response (sleeplessness or insomnia), which in turn produced a behavioral response (problems in school). On one hand, this interconnectedness can be massively overwhelming.

On the other hand, if a grieving person addresses just one of his or her grief responses, this change has a significant ripple effect. The griever begins to feel better in many ways.

Caring for Your Body

Many people find that taking care of themselves physically is the most immediate and concrete kind of grief work they can do. Grieving people should try hard to exercise, sleep well, and eat nutritiously.

Get Active!

Physical exercise has enormous health benefits. Exercise is also a wonderful stress reliever. When you exercise, your body produces chemicals called endorphins, which create a state of relaxation in the body. Here are some suggestions for incorporating exercise into your daily routine:

- Walk or ride your bike whenever possible, instead of relying on rides.
- Continue any organized sports you may be participating in. Don't drop out.
- Exercise with friends or family members. Grab a companion and your skateboard, scooter, or bike.
- Go to a park, gym, or swimming pool, instead of watching television or playing computer games.

Grief Journal Exercise: *Keep a log of how much you exercise each day, and rate your level of exercise as "great," "fair," or "needs work." If you aren't exercising enough, draw up an Exercise Plan. List your favorite kinds of exercise, the days you'll exercise, and how long you'll exercise each day. Add the names of friends who might join you.*

More Good News About Exercise

Exercise is good for your emotional health, too. It reduces anxiety and depression. Exercise also builds self-confidence, improves concentration, and boosts energy levels.

Sleep Well

Many people suffering a loss have sleep problems or insomnia. Sleep deprivation, in turn, contributes to daytime fatigue, problems in concentration, and feelings of being over-whelmed. Although insomnia is a normal part of grief, you can take active steps to get a good night's sleep:

- Establish a routine bedtime that will allow you to unwind and send a signal to your brain that it's time to sleep.
- Try some helpful bedtime rituals, such as drinking warm milk, taking a hot bath, or reading.

- Promote good sleep through daily exercise. Avoid strenuous exercise within three hours before bedtime.
- Avoid caffeine found in coffee, tea, sodas, and chocolate, especially in the afternoon and evening.
- Try to stay up during the day and avoid naps. Naps throw your sleep schedule off and make it harder to fall asleep at your regular bedtime.
- If you wake and can't fall back to sleep, leave your bedroom and try a relaxing activity elsewhere, such as listening to soothing music or reading. Return to bed when you feel drowsy.

Grief Journal Exercise: *Keep a sleep log and rate your sleep as "great," "fair," or "needs work." List the strategies you'll try to improve your sleep. Try this plan for a week and then reevaluate.*

Eat Healthy Foods

Altered eating patterns are a normal response to grief. Some people who are grieving lose their appetite and forget to eat, causing mood swings and fatigue induced by low blood sugar. Other people overeat, using food for comfort. Unfortunately, sugary snacks and the carbohydrates in comfort food, such as pasta and white bread, later induce a "sugar crash," along with tiredness, irritability, and depression.

Watch your own eating patterns for changes. Here are some ideas for healthy eating as you grieve:

- Eat three nutritious meals a day. If you can't eat three regular meals, eat five small ones.
- Make yourself nutritious smoothies in the blender. Add yogurt, bananas, and other healthy ingredients.
- Avoid snacking on junk food.
- Drink at least four or five glasses of water a day.
- Keep healthy food, like fruits and vegetables, nearby.
- If you see that your eating patterns continue to change, tell a parent or doctor. You may need some help returning to a healthy diet.

Grief Journal Exercise: Write down what you eat for a week to find out if your eating patterns have changed. If there are changes, outline the steps you'll take to bring your eating habits back to your more typical pattern. Be sure to include the names of people who can help you get back on track. Keep a log for a week and then reevaluate.

Four

Express Your
FEELINGS

David and Brian were identical twins. They shared a bedroom, as well as a love for the Boston Red Sox, chocolate-chip cookies, and computer games. The day after the twins turned twelve, Brian was injured while playing base-ball. He sustained head injuries and went into a coma. Brian died several days later.

David felt like a part of himself had died, too. At school, he sought out his friends, desperately pretending he was all right. He developed stomach cramps and muscle pains. Sometimes David dreamed his brother was still alive and he woke up drenched in sweat. David was filled with feelings that he couldn't understand, much less express.

One day in art class, David got out the paints. As he spread colors over the page, he thought of Brian. His drawings were just senseless swirls. After all, David reflected, his brother's dying made no sense, either.

After that, David began to paint at home. Through his painting, he released his feelings of confusion and loss. He hung his pictures over Brian's bed. Although he didn't know it then, David was taking the first step toward healing.

How Expressing Your Feelings Helps

Grief hurts. Many grieving people, their bodies weak and their minds dazed, don't know what to do with the painful emotions they're feeling. The best thing to do with feelings is to express them.

Expressing the emotions of grief helps by providing a release. If you've ever made microwave popcorn, you know how the hot kernels begin to push against the bag until the bag actually shakes. People's feelings are the same way. Like the bursting kernels in the popcorn bag, intense feelings clamor to be set free. That's why people talk about "getting things off their chest." Their burden becomes lighter.

After her mother was killed by a drunk driver, eleven-year-old Angela walked around feeling numb. "People said, 'you should talk about it.' How could I talk about it when I didn't even know what I was feeling myself?" Angela asks. "I just felt tense all the time."

Angela was unaware that she was taking out her feelings on the people around her. She was irritable and snapped at friends for no reason. She often started arguments with her sister. After she exploded, Angela felt better, never realizing that the fights were her way of venting deeper feelings about her mother's death.

One day, in a calm moment, Angela started talking with her sister about her mother's accident. "All of a sudden, my feelings came pouring out," she remembers. "I realized I was sad but also really, really angry. It helped to know what I was feeling. I didn't feel so heavy anymore."

Now Angela and her sister have their mother's photograph in the dining room and talk about her often. Angela swims laps to release some of her rage, and has donated her allowance money to Mothers Against Drunk Driving. Her anger has not gone away, but it has diminished.

Keep Talking
Ryan's brother died of AIDS when Ryan was twelve. For weeks after the funeral, Ryan shrugged when people asked how he was doing. Finally, the school counselor took Ryan aside and urged him to talk.

Ryan admitted that he thought that talking about his brother's death would just make him feel worse. The counselor assured him that keeping feelings bottled up is what makes people feel worse. Although most people fear that they'll fall apart when they express sadness or anger, what usually happens is that—even if they cry or yell— they can pull themselves together and feel a great sense of relief afterward.

Like Ryan, many grieving people are afraid to talk about their feelings. It helps to pick one or two people you'd feel most comfortable confiding in. If a parent has died and the remaining parent is absorbed with his or her own pain, choose someone else on your Support Team. Later on, your parent may be ready to help shoulder the grieving.

Grief Journal Exercise: *List the people you will talk with about how you're feeling. You may want to decide which three people you'll talk with first and when you'll approach these people.*

Friends can be an important source of comfort. Often, young people like Ryan fear that friends will feel sorry for them or treat them differently. In an effort to fit in, many grieving teens try to hide their feelings. Take a risk. When you mention how bad you've been feeling, you may be surprised by your friends' genuine support. If friends can't be there for you, you may want to try other ways to get help from people your own age (see Chapter 5).

When Words Fail

Kristen's mother was diagnosed with breast cancer when Kristen was ten years old. After the diagnosis, her mother's doctor started her on chemotherapy, a treatment for cancer that kills cancer cells.

"We thought she was getting better," recalls Kristen. "At first, she lost all her hair from the chemo, but then it grew back. We were all so relieved. We even laughed about the little turban she wore while she was getting the treatments." It wasn't long, however, before the doctors found a tumor on her liver. She went into the hospital, where she died.

Kristen's grief was overwhelming. "We did everything together," Kristen remembers. "We used to play duets together on the piano, and we went to the mall together—we even brushed our teeth together." Kristen couldn't cry. "I kind of turned to stone, I guess," says Kristen.

The first weeks after Kristen's mother died, Kristen's father worked at his computer, tormented by his own grief. Her younger brother and sister stayed in day care for longer hours. The house was empty. Kristen returned to school but

ANTICIPATORY GRIEVING: WHEN DEATH IS ON THE WAY

When twelve-year-old Roger's grandfather moved to a hospice, a homelike center for dying people, Roger had to prepare for his first visit there. His grandfather was dying of end-stage liver cancer, and Roger felt frightened, sad, and confused all at the same time. He was experiencing anticipatory grief, the normal grief that occurs when a person is expecting a death.

Anticipatory grief can include the emotional, physical, and behavioral reactions that are part of grief after a death has occurred. Preparing for a person's death gives the griever a chance to say good-bye and conclude any unfinished business. Watching the dying person suffer, however, can be unbearable. If someone close to you is dying, here are some ways you can grieve:

- Be prepared before you visit. Get information about the patient's medical condition and visible differences, such as changes in hair, skin, or weight. It helps to know what to expect.

- Bring flowers or a small gift to connect with the person who is dying.
- Think of what you want to say ahead of time. Share news of your life, reminiscences, or ways you want to say thank you or good-bye.
- Visit with an adult or other family member for support.
- Make sure you have someone you can talk to if your visit does not go as planned (for example, the dying person is in pain or is heavily medicated).

Roger decided to take his father along for the first visit to his grandfather's hospice. He brought a pot of bright red tulips and a photo of his new hamster. The nurses prepared Roger with information that his grandfather had lost a lot of weight. During his visit, Roger sat beside his grandfather's bed and told him stories about his new hamster. Roger's grandfather was pleased that Roger had come. Although Roger felt sad after he left, he was glad he'd visited. He knew he would go again.

avoided her friends. Then, one day, her piano teacher asked her to play one of the pieces she'd practiced with her mother. "That did it," says Kristen. "I felt my heart break into a million pieces. As I played the duet, I sobbed and sobbed. I guess that was the first day I actually let some of my feelings out."

For Kristen, the music and a relationship with a trusted teacher finally freed her to express her feelings and begin to feel better. Like Kristen, some people have trouble expressing their grief in words. Often, these people did not verbalize their feelings much even before the death occurred. Here are some ways—beyond words—to express your feelings:

- Keep a journal. Start a special notebook, a private place where you can record your feelings, keep photographs, or draw pictures as often as you like.
- Read books whose main characters are grieving. Try *A Summer to Die* by Lois Lowry, *Bridge to Terabithia* by Katherine Paterson, *Missing May* by Cynthia Rylant, and *Charlotte's Web* by E. B. White. Reading about someone else's grief can help put you in touch with your own feelings.
- Do some exercises in a grief workbook. (Several workbooks are listed in the back of this book.)
- Let music bring out your feelings. If you play an instrument, try pieces that help you tap into your feelings. Listen to music that elicits feelings.

- Work with clay, either in an art class or at home. For some people, sculpting seems to free up feelings.
- Paint with pastels or oils, or try drawing or sketching. What is important is not just the picture, but the feelings that the art releases.

Grief Journal Exercise: *If you're not comfortable talking with people, write down the other ways you might try expressing your feelings.*

Five

Reaching OUT

Alisha thought she had the best father in the world. He had taught her how to ride a bike, catch fly balls, and whistle. Suddenly, when Alisha was thirteen, her father was diagnosed with pancreatic cancer. Ten weeks later—the day before Father's Day—her father died. Alisha was consumed with grief. "He was the best father in the world... and he was dead," she said.

She began skipping school because she felt too depressed to get up. She withdrew from her friends and quit the softball team. When Alisha broke down sobbing in class one day, her guidance counselor suggested she get help from a therapist who specialized in helping young people. Alisha's mother took her to her first counseling session.

The therapist listened while Alisha talked about her father's cancer and the Father's Day card she never gave him. As Alisha began to sob, her mother put her arm around her and they cried together.

Alisha saw the therapist every week. At first, Alisha just poured out her sadness while the therapist listened. Then Alisha got in touch with her anger. She was angry that her father had died so young and wouldn't share her life as she grew up. He wouldn't be at her sixteenth birthday, her prom, or her graduation. The therapist provided a safe haven where Alisha could explore her feelings and feel accepted. After six months, Alisha felt much better. She had reconnected with her old friends and made some new ones.

"My therapist made a huge difference," reflects Alisha. "She was there for me, no matter what. In the beginning, I was nervous and worried that I wouldn't know how to be in counseling, but she said that was her job. Deciding to see a therapist was one of the best decisions I ever made."

Who Should Seek Help

Often, despite our best efforts, the symptoms of grief do not diminish. Anyone who is suffering through a time of grief should consider working with a therapist if he or she is experiencing:

- Ongoing sleeplessness
- Changes in appetite and weight
- Thoughts of killing oneself
- Isolation from friends and family
- Poor performance in school
- Consistent feelings of sadness
- Feeling numb or unable to touch the feelings inside
- No interest in activities that once provided satisfaction

***Grief Journal Exercise:** If you would like to try getting professional support, make a list of the adults who could help you find a counselor. Decide which person you'll talk with first, along with a day and time when you'll approach this person. You might even want to write down your opening sentence to help you get started.*

What to Expect

Having a therapist is like having a coach to help you as you grieve. The therapist has special skills to help you deal with mixed emotions about the person who died or with lingering feelings of anger and guilt. Besides listening, your therapist may offer concrete ideas about how to take care of yourself physically or how to reach out to family and friends. Some therapists will suggest books or journal exercises to help you between sessions.

If you're considering therapy, ask your parent or another adult to help you find someone to talk with. Often the best way to find a therapist is through friends who have had a positive experience with that person. Recommendations from your teachers, school psychologist, or family doctor are also good places to start.

There are many kinds of therapists who can help you with your grief. *School psychologists* work in the schools, often with entire classrooms or with groups of students. They may meet with grieving students or suggest someone in the community who can help. *Clergy,* including ministers, priests, and rabbis, devote time to help the members of their congregations with psychological problems. They often bring a spiritual approach to their counseling.

Social workers are professionals who may have had special training in family counseling or loss issues. *Psychologists* can diagnose and treat emotional problems, and may also have special grief-work skills. *Grief or bereavement counselors* specialize in grieving and often work at hospices, hospitals, and grief centers. Finally, *psychiatrists* are medical doctors who can prescribe medications and sometimes offer therapy as well.

Grief or Depression?

In the early weeks after their loss, most grieving people feel depressed. Brought on by loss, this depression is sometimes called bereavement depression. While depression caused by grief tends to lift over time, clinical depression does not. Unlike grief, clinical depression includes feelings of hopelessness, helplessness, and poor self-esteem. Rabbi Earl A. Grollman writes:

Grief says, "How can I go on?"

Depression cries, "Why go on?"

Grief says, "Will I ever laugh again?"

Depression cries, "There is no laughter."

If, after awhile, your grief has not lessened, you may be suffering from depression, which can be treated. If you—or someone close to you—thinks you are suffering from depression, see a professional for help.

When you meet your therapist, ask questions about how he or she works with young people who are grieving. After a few sessions, you will know if you can relax with this person and feel comfortable talking about your feelings. Grief work can be much easier with a good therapist at your side.

Other Ways of Getting Help

Some people find help in other ways. If you have access

THE RISK OF SUICIDE

Twelve-year-old Anna was in the backseat of a car her sister was driving when the car was hit by a speeding truck. The medics rescued Anna from the burning car, and she watched as her dead sister was pulled from the wreckage.

Anna fell apart. She had nightmares about the burning car and woke up screaming. As the weeks passed, Anna became listless and depressed. She stayed in bed for days at a time and went to school only when her mother noticed she'd been absent.

Nothing really mattered anymore, Anna thought. She began to wish she were dead. One day, Anna took her mother's sleeping pills from the medicine cabinet. In math class, Anna told her girlfriend, Joan, that she was going to swallow the bottle of pills that evening. "I'll be with my sister by nine tonight," she said. Anna made her friend promise not to tell anyone.

Joan wanted to keep her word but worried that Anna really would kill herself. Joan told her math teacher, who, in turn, told the school psychologist. The psychologist called Anna's parents, who came to school. The psychologist set up an evaluation with a crisis team at a nearby hospital.

The crisis team placed Anna in a hospital for three days. She met her therapist there and started an anti-depressant medication to help reduce her negative thoughts. With her therapist, Anna began to talk—for the first time—about the horror of her sister's death. Over time, Anna's wish to die went away, and although she still missed her sister, she began to feel better.

If you are having thoughts about ending your life, you should get help immediately. If your friend is thinking of hurting himself or herself, you should tell an adult, even if your friend has asked you not to.

The warning signs for suicide risk are:

- Continuous or persistent talk about wanting to join the deceased
- Increased reckless behavior
- A sudden change in attention to appearance
- Giving away possessions
- Talking about wanting to die, especially with specific details
- Withdrawal from friends
- Substance abuse

If you have no one to talk to, call the toll-free National Suicide Hotline at 800-SUICIDE (800-784-2433).

Grief Journal Exercise: *Are you think-ing of getting help but fear is holding you back? If so, make a list of your fears and consider if each one is realistic. If you still feel stuck, make two columns in your journal: "What I Have to Lose by Trying Counseling" and "What I Have to Gain by Trying Counseling." See how these lists stack up.*

to the Internet, you may sign up for an online chat room or club specifically designed for grieving young people. The back of this book lists several such groups. You can participate in a prearranged chat time or exchange e-mails with other young people who are grieving.

Support groups that deal with grief and loss are another valuable source of help. They are offered by hospitals, mental-health centers, and grief organizations. Support groups allow members to talk about feelings in a safe and accepting environment. Many grieving people find great comfort in talking with people who've "been there."

Twelve-year-old Michael attended a support group after the death of his grandmother, who had been suffering from Alzheimer's disease. Even though he didn't want to go at first, Michael gave in at the urging of his minister.

"At first, I said, 'Forget it. Who wants to sit around with a bunch of other kids who are miserable like me?'" recalls Michael. "But I went anyway, just to please my minister. At the group, we took turns talking about who had died and what we felt like, stuff like that. Then we gave each other ideas about how to handle our situations. The other kids were cool, and they knew what I was talking about because they'd been through the same thing. And one time, we did some special exercises about saying good-bye that really helped me."

Six

Keeping Memories ALIVE

Well-known grief educator and author Dr. Alan Wolfelt writes, "When someone you love dies, the person lives on in you through memory…Good memories from life help soften painful feelings of death. When you keep these memories alive, you keep the person you loved alive inside you, too."

Creating and cherishing memories is called commemorating. People commemorate in many ways. They often participate in public rituals, such as funerals or memorial services. People can also preserve their memories through private activities. Because commemorating helps us stay connected to the deceased, it is the heart of healing.

Funerals and Memorial Services

Each religious tradition has its own set of rituals for honoring the dead. These rituals are important because they allow those who are grieving a chance to acknowledge the death and to say good-bye. These traditions are also ways that people can remember and celebrate the life of the departed.

In most Christian religions, a funeral director takes the body of the deceased to a funeral home to arrange for burial. The body may be embalmed, using chemicals to make the person look alive. An embalmed body is placed in a casket, which can be simple or elaborate. For one to three days preceding the burial, the body is displayed in a closed or open casket at the funeral home. This is called a visitation or wake. A wake is an ancient ritual rooted in earlier times when people kept watch over the body to be sure the person was not buried alive. Today, it is a chance for mourners to comfort one another and reminisce about the life of the deceased.

After the wake, a member of the clergy performs the funeral service, which may be held at a church, gravesite, or funeral home. Often these services include prayers, music, and stories about the deceased. Today, growing numbers of people are choosing cremation rather than a traditional burial. Cremation means that the body is burned and the ashes are preserved or scattered in a meaningful place.

Jewish people follow a specific set of mourning customs that are rich with meaning. Before the funeral, a rabbi tears a black ribbon pinned to the mourners garments. This practice is called tearing the keriah. It allows the mourner to express anguish and anger.

After the burial, mourners recite the Kaddish, a powerful prayer that focuses on life, not death. The Kaddish is recited every day for eleven months by a grieving parent and for thirty days by other family members. The Kaddish is also recited on the anniversary of the death.

Upon returning from the cemetery, the family follows the old custom of "sitting shiva," a seven-day period of mourning. *Shiva* means "seven" in Hebrew and was first mentioned in the Book of Genesis, when Joseph mourned his father, Jacob, for seven days. Throughout the seven days of shiva, family members and friends come to the home of the bereaved to offer condolences. Shiva allows the mourners to focus their complete attention on grieving and to comfort one another. Shiva ends the morning of the seventh day. The mourners take a walk around the block as a way of reentering the world.

Some bereaved people, particularly those who do not adhere to a religious tradition, often create their own memorial service. Memorial services may include music and readings chosen by those who knew the deceased, as well as time for

Festivals to Honor the Dead

Some cultures commemorate the dead yearly through colorful festivals. In Mexico, November 1 and 2 are called the Days of the Dead, when the deceased are said to return home. People make altars in their homes in memory of their deceased relatives. They decorate the altars with photographs of the departed as well as the deceased's favorite food and drink. During these festival days, markets sell chocolate skulls, sugar coffins, and bread shaped like bones. Families gather at cemeteries to clean the graves and then decorate them with candles, incense, and crosses of red and yellow marigolds. Bells are rung to summon the dead spirits. People feast near the graves, sometimes celebrating with fireworks and the music of mariachi bands.

In midsummer, the Japanese celebrate O-Bon, the Festival of the Dead, three days in which ancestors are believed to pay a visit. Family members return to their hometowns. At gravesites, people light small bonfires and hang paper lanterns to guide the spirits home. In the evening, families have a big feast of summer dishes, including sushi and green-tea ice cream. On the grounds of a temple, people of all ages dance a solemn Dance of the Dead, called Bon-Odori, which is believed to send the deceased back after their visit home.

In Jamaica, mourners hold a festival each time a person dies. The celebration of Nine Nights is held to bid the deceased farewell and to ensure a safe journey into the next world. The festival usually takes place in a tent or bamboo veranda and includes singing, reading Bible passages, reciting prayers, telling stories about the deceased, and playing games such as dominoes. There is much dancing. People drink coffee and rum and eat fried fish and hard bread. At daybreak after the ninth night, Jamaicans believe that the deceased is free, and the ceremony ends.

participants to reflect on their own memories of the person who has died. Memorial services allow the community of grievers to celebrate the life of the deceased.

The Importance of Funerals

Funerals and memorial services help by:
- *Enforcing the reality of the death*
- *Providing an opportunity for expressing grief*
- *Allowing participants to honor the life of the deceased*
- *Offering a way for friends and family to support one another*

Other Ways to Commemorate

Spend some private time. Some people create their own ways to honor the deceased, such as spending time in nature reflecting on the deceased person, sharing quiet time with a pet, visiting the gravesite, lighting a memorial candle, and listening to music that evokes memories of the deceased.

Create something. Many people make memorials, which are visual ways to keep their memories alive. Collect favorite photographs of the deceased and make a collage or scrapbook. The scrapbook could include a copy of the memorial service and quotes from people who knew the deceased.

Put together a decorated "memory box" containing treasured objects that belonged to the deceased person, including photos, letters, ticket stubs, or anything else that reminds you of the person who died. Keep a memento that belonged to the deceased, such as jewelry or a favorite piece of clothing.

Tell stories. Sharing stories and jokes about the departed is an age-old way of keeping memories alive.

Write it down. Many people write stories, poems, or recollections about the person who has died in a journal or memory book. Others find solace in writing a letter to the person who has died. You could even try writing a play about the person's life, or cowriting a story about the person who died with a parent, sibling, or friend.

Grief Journal Exercise: List the ways you have commemorated your loved one so far, including both public and private ways of remembering. Then record the ways you plan to commemorate the deceased in the future.

Make the memories matter. Many grieving people take some action or create a "living memorial," which ensures that the work or values of the deceased person live on. If the person died from an illness, you may want to learn more about that illness and make a donation to an organization that is working to cure that illness. You could volunteer for a community agency that was important to the deceased or do a good deed in honor of the person who has died.

When Laurie was thirteen, her stepmother was diagnosed with kidney failure caused by diabetes. She died the following year. In the early stages of her grief, Laurie preserved the memories of her stepmother by displaying a photograph by her bed and by wearing the ring her stepmother had left her. As the weeks passed, Laurie began to think about how her stepmother had died of diabetes because no cure was available. In the fall, she signed up for the

Walk to Cure Diabetes. Along with her Girl Scout troop, she and her father participated in the walk together.

"I cried at times, during the walk," Laurie remembers. "But it was good crying. My dad was walking right beside me, and so were my friends and all these other people, supporting a cure. I didn't feel alone. And because of something I did, my stepmother lived on. I made a difference in honor of her."

Seven

Moving ON

Thirteen-year-old Greg and his best friend, Matt, loved the Beatles. After school, they'd often listen to their favorite Beatles songs, singing to the lyrics. Then, one day, Matt was killed in a bike accident. Greg thought he'd never be able to listen to another Beatles song again.

About a year later, Greg turned on a Beatles tape. He waited for the stabbing feeling, the ache of regret. It wasn't there. Instead, Greg felt a softer sadness. He felt a fondness for his friend, not a frantic missing. Greg was beginning to heal.

Author and grief expert Helen Fitzgerald has worked with hundreds of grieving young people like Greg. She offers the following clues that indicate that, if you've been grieving, you are beginning to feel better:

- Your sleeping, eating, and exercising patterns return to normal.
- You no longer feel tired all the time.
- You can remember the deceased without crying or feeling intense sadness.
- You can hear music the deceased listened to without feeling pain.
- You can concentrate on homework, television, or a movie.
- Some time passes when you are not thinking about the deceased.
- You can enjoy a party or a good joke without feeling guilty.
- You can look forward to holidays or vacations.
- You can reach out to someone else who is grieving.

Some people worry that feeling better is a betrayal of the person they've lost. It may help to remember that the deceased would want you to carry on with your life. Other people fear that feeling better means they are starting to forget the deceased. In fact, people begin to feel better because they remember the person who has died by honoring that person in their lives. They have included some of the memories and values of that person they loved in the way that they live every day. In this manner, the deceased person lives on.

Holidays and Anniversaries

Even when people are feeling better, they often feel sad and upset during holidays, particularly during the first year after the death of a loved one. Revived signs of grief, including physical, emotional, and behavioral signs, are all normal. The anniversary of the person's death and the birthday of the deceased can be especially hard. Other difficult holidays are Mother's Day, Father's Day, Christmas and Hanukkah, Thanksgiving, New Year's Day, and Valentine's Day.

It can help to make plans ahead of time about how you and your family will spend an upcoming holiday. The holidays are best handled by acknowledging the sadness and loss they can bring.

There are many ways to commemorate the deceased on a holiday:

- Light a candle at Thanksgiving or other significant meal.
- If you celebrate Hanukkah, recall a special memory of the person for each night you light the menorah. If you celebrate Christmas, talk about the ornaments that bring back memories of the deceased. Place pine boughs, lights, or decorations around the person's photograph.
- On the anniversary of the deceased person's death, visit the grave, plant a garden, or read some poems.
- At the holiday meal, prepare food that the deceased person loved or donate this dish to a soup kitchen.

- At the holiday meal or gathering, listen to music that the deceased person enjoyed.
- Display the photograph collages, quilts, and memory boxes you made in the early days of your grieving.
- On the deceased's birthday, or any other special holiday, work at a shelter or do some other good deed in memory of that person.

A Meal of Condolence

A Jewish ritual called the meal of condolence carries a valuable lesson for all bereaved people. According to Jewish custom, the first meal after the burial of a loved one is prepared and served by friends of the mourners to help them regain their strength. The meal includes lentils, bread, and hard-boiled eggs, all of which are associated with life in the Jewish faith. The mourners eat hard-boiled eggs to affirm life in the face of death. The egg hardens as it cooks and symbolizes the mourners' determination to endure through tragedy.

Ever since his father died of skin cancer last year, twelve-year-old Max reads the obituaries in the newspaper. "At the end of the article, it always says that the dead person is 'survived by' and lists who's left," says Max. "That always gets to me. I am a survivor! It's like I survived a flood or a car crash—but worse. Much, much worse."

If you have lost someone you love, you are indeed a survivor. You have survived the most difficult disaster of all. Grieving may be one of the hardest things you'll ever do.

Grieving people often report that their grief has changed them. Their loss has taught them many lessons. They know they have the tools to face any challenge life brings. Many people experience a new compassion for others who are grieving. They have a new appreciation of life and live each day to its fullest.

These people, who have weathered grief and endured, offer words of advice to people new to grieving. They speak of hope, and report that the healing does begin and the grief does lift.

If you are still suffering from intense grief, you may not believe that you will learn or grow from your loss. The possibility of hope may seem remote indeed. Because you may never have experienced grief, you may never have known the process of healing, either. You may feel more hopeful as the healing begins in your own life.

You have sustained an enormous loss. You have lived through the worst disaster of all. You are bearing the un-bearable. Every day that you take the smallest of steps to feel better is a victory. From time to time, you may get a glimpse of your own resilience. You are a survivor, doing the best you can. You have reason to be proud.

GLOSSARY

anticipatory grief: response to the loss of a person suffering from a prolonged illness who has not yet died

bereavement: the way a person expresses grief

bereavement counselor: a therapist trained to work with grieving people

commemorate: to keep alive the memories of a deceased person

depression: continuing sadness that does not lift two months after the death; symptoms of depression include fatigue, difficulty maintaining a daily routine, insomnia, a sense of helplessness, and despair

endorphins: chemicals made by the brain, which are stimulated by exercise; endorphins produce feelings of relaxation and are known to reduce stress

express feelings: to move feelings from the inside of the person, where they are private, to the outside, where they take on a new form, such as art or conversation grief: a normal response to loss

grief work: the actions taken to confront the feelings of grief and to feel better

guilt: the feeling that one is responsible for an action—in this case, death

memorial: a work of art, such as a photograph, painting, or poem, that honors the person who has died

memorial service: a gathering of family and friends to commemorate the person who has died

mourning: the outward expression of grief

psychiatrist: a medical doctor who is trained to help people cope and who is able to prescribe medication

psychologist: a mental-health counselor who can help people who are grieving

ritual: a specific series of actions done with an intended meaning—in this case, to honor the deceased

shiva: the seven-day period of mourning prescribed by Jewish custom

tasks of grief: the steps designed to help a grieving person confront grief and to move on

FURTHER RESOURCES

Books

Dower, Laura. *I Will Remember You: What to Do When Someone You Love Dies*. New York: HarperCollins, 2001.

Fitzgerald, Helen. *The Grieving Teen: A Guide for Teenagers and Their Friends*. New York: Fireside, 2000.

Gootman, Marilyn E. *When a Friend Dies: A Book for Teens About Grieving & Healing*. Minneapolis: Free Spirit Publishing, 1994.

Grollman, Earl A. *Straight Talk About Death for Teenagers: How to Cope with Losing Someone You Love*. Boston: Beacon Press, 1993.

Krementz, Jill. *How It Feels When a Parent Dies*. New York: Alfred A. Knopf, 1988.

Workbooks

Mayo, Peg Elliott. *The Healing Sorrow Workbook: Rituals for Transforming Grief and Loss*. Oakland, Calif.: New Harbinger Publications, 2001.

Salloum, Alison, *Reactions: A Workbook to Help Young People Who Are Experiencing Trauma and Grief*. Omaha, Neb.: Centering Corp., 1998.

Samuel Traisman, Enid. *Fire in My Heart, Ice in My Veins: A Journal for Teenagers Experiencing a Loss.* Omaha, Neb.: Centering Corp., 1992.

Shavatt, Donna, and Eve Shavatt. *My Grieving Journey Book.* New York: Paulist Press, 2002.

CD-ROMs and Videos

These videos can be purchased online at www.brossia-marsh.com/aftercare.html#videotapes.

The Courage to Grieve, The Courage to Grow. Features grief expert Judy Tatelbaum, MSW. Includes information on how to recognize grief and steps to take to relieve it (45 minutes).

Feelings. Discusses the normal feelings that are part of grief (11 minutes).

Saying Good-Bye (Teen Version). Explores feelings of grief and gives suggestions for commemorations (34 minutes).

A Time to Live—A Time to Die. Follows a teenage girl who learns to cope with the death of her father (41 minutes).

Understanding Grief—Kids Helping Kids. Sensitive film designed for viewers aged nine to fourteen. Children who have actually lost someone through death discuss their feelings (14 minutes).

Related Online Sites

Community of Daughters
www.communityofdaughters.net
This Web site is designed to bring women and girls together who have endured the loss of a parent. Members can tell their story and read the stories of others.

GriefNet
www.griefnet.org
GriefNet is an Internet community of people dealing with grief, death, and major loss. It offers e-mail support groups and articles about grieving.

HospiceNet
www.hospicenet.org/index.html
Hospice Net provides information and support to patients and families facing life-threatening illnesses. It also provides a wealth of material about grieving.

Kidsaid
kidsaid.com
This is an online support group for young people. It provides a chance to offer and receive support via e-mail with people of a similar age and experience.

The Grieving Child
www.grievingchild.org
This Web site offers information for children based on their age, including activities to help children cope. The site also helps locate the nearest grieving center in your area.

Index

ABOUT THE AUTHOR

Carol Antoinette Peacock is a practicing psychologist and writer. She has worked with grieving young people for more than thirty years. As director of a group home for adolescents, she led loss groups for teens. In her current practice, she specializes in treating families and children. Her co-therapist is her black Labrador, Pepper.

Dr. Peacock has written extensively about how children experience loss. Her book about mother-daughter separation, *Hand Me Down Dreams,* was followed by a children's book on diabetes, *Sugar Was My Best Food: Diabetes and Me.* In 2000, Dr. Peacock wrote *Mommy Far, Mommy Near: An Adoption Story,* which was named a 2001 Notable Social Studies Trade Book for Young People. She is also the author of a picture book, *Pilgrim Cat.*

Dr. Peacock has degrees from Cornell University, Columbia School for Social Work, and Boston College. She lives outside Boston with her husband, Tom Gagen, as well as her stepson, Jonathan, and her daughters, Elizabeth and Katherine.

U.S. $6.95

Of all the losses imaginable, death is the most final and often the hardest to bear. Many people who suffer this loss for the first time are frightened by their grief and may try to avoid it, but grieving is a necessary part of starting to feel better. In this "guidebook" for grieving, child psychologist Carol Antoinette Peacock describes simple, specific actions that help to ease the pain. Readers will also find ideas for expressing their feelings and keeping the memories alive, paving the way to a new life.

Life Balance navigates the challenges of everyday life. Featuring real-life situations and helpful resources, each book gives readers the tools they need to make positive changes and smart decisions. Filled with facts, advice, and solutions, Life Balance is about finding the way to a healthy—and happy—life.

Other Books in This Series:

ADHD	Family Therapy	Reaching Your Goals
Date Violence	Healthy Sexuality	School Conflict
Depression	Intelligence	Schizophrenia
Dreams and Sleep	Keeping a Journal	Therapy
Dyslexia	Meditation	Yoga
Eating Disorders	Phobias	
Emotional Intelligence	Prejudice	

ISBN 0-531-16728-3